THE ADVENTURES OF

Hamish McMoosie

❧

HAMISH McMOOSIE AND THE LONG, HARD WINTER

❧

This book belongs to

Dedication

This book is dedicated to children everywhere
and to those who love the magic of Christmas

Published 2003 by Waverley Books, David Dale House,
New Lanark, ML11 9DJ, Scotland

Copyright © Text – Terry Isaac 2003

Copyright © Illustrations – Mandi Madden 2003

The right of Terry Isaac to be identified as the author of this
work has been asserted by him in accordance with the
Copyright, Designs and Patents Act 1988

A CIP catalogue record for this book is available from the British Library

ISBN 1 902407 31 8

Printed and bound in Poland

Designed and typeset by twelveotwo

Hamish McMoosie

HAMISH McMOOSIE AND THE LONG, HARD WINTER

TERRY ISAAC

ILLUSTRATED BY MANDI MADDEN

WAVERLEY
BOOKS

Hamish McMoosie's paw traced patterns on the frosted glass of the window of the tiny, cosy cottage, he shared with his wife Dorma, hidden deep under the steps of the old house which had stood right next to the cathedral in the very old city for many hundreds of years.

The first snows of winter had arrived, in flurries and scurries driven by the north wind, and had left crisp, cold, snowy tam o' shanters* iced onto the rooftops, and an icy white quilt covering the slumbering earth beneath. The wind, being the north wind, carried the snow south to Edinburgh and beyond. Hamish smiled a contented smile. Christmas was just a twinkling star away.

*A tam o' shanter is a large, Scottish flat cap.

Hamish, continuing to draw little stars and Christmas trees on the frosted window pane, was deep in thought because tomorrow night he would lead the congregation in the carol service by playing his beloved bagpipes at the candlelit midnight gathering held in the cathedral. It was a very important event. Dorma, his wife, would be sitting in her usual place. Then Hamish remembered – his finicky Aunt Maude would be there too with her long, black umbrella with the goose-head handle and sharp pointed end! Aunt Maude had the habit of poking her umbrella in Hamish's rear whenever she felt annoyed with him, which, unfortunately for Hamish, was often.

Oh why, oh why, thought Hamish, did Dorma have to spoil Christmas by inviting Aunt Maude to stay?

Hamish recalled Dorma had been doing very odd things lately. She was buying all sorts of towels – mostly white, when Hamish knew that the linen cupboard was stacked to the roof – and as for the Christmas food preparations, well, Hamish thought that was enough to feed an army of mice.

This year, by September, Dorma had all her spice-perfumed Christmas puddings made and by October the larder shelf was heavy with two rich, dark fruitcakes snuggled together and maturing, waiting to be woken to wear their festive coats of marzipan and icing. By November, the marble shelf in the larder almost groaned aloud under the extra weight of meat pies maturing away. There were game pies with rich, savoury jelly holding the meats inside the crisp, crusty pastry and some pork pies very happily slumbering and improving in taste. Dorma had to keep a very careful eye on the pork pies as Hamish had been known in the past to take a sample or two as a midnight feast.

Last week, Dorma had even asked that Hamish decorate the tall Christmas pine that he had cut with his axe from the forest nearby. The decoration of the tree was a task that Dorma had always done herself.

There were so many things that were not quite normal. Dorma would always let Hamish help put the small decorations on the icing after it has set hard. Hamish liked to make little Christmas scenes with the decorations and Hamish always made a good job in doing so. However, this year Hamish found, while quietly sniffing at a pork pie, just to make sure it was doing OK, that the cakes were ready – all glistening with a hard white icing and little Christmassy scenes. He knew the icing was hard because he prodded at it with a paw.

Dorma had her Christmas list pinned up on the noticeboard that she had managed, with a lot of coaxing, to get Hamish to put up on one of the walls in the kitchen. Hamish, as you might expect, was no master craftsman when it came to doing odd jobs around the house. He had never got the noticeboard to hang quite right, and for years it had hung on the wall at an odd angle. Hamish did, from time to time, say that he would unscrew the board and put it back correctly, but Dorma very kindly said that the board had become a feature of her kitchen and it was best left as it was. She was not quite certain that if Hamish did take it down that it would in fact go back up correctly, if at all. Most likely, all that would happen would be that Hamish would bang himself on the thumb with the hammer – which is what happened the first time he tried to put the noticeboard up on the wall. The board would be left well alone.

On the list, which hung on the noticeboard, Dorma kept a note of all the things that had to be done before Christmas. Most of the reminders had been crossed out and only a few remained . . . those that Hamish had to do!

Dorma was standing sipping a cup of tea and looking at the list. She hummed contentedly to herself as she read down the crossed-out reminders. She told herself all was progressing nicely.

Her eyes reached the bottom of the list where Hamish's "To Do" things were written. Dorma smiled and sipped her tea. Hamish was Hamish, and she knew that after a wee bit of reminding, and a lot of last-minute rushing around, her husband would get his "To Do" things done. It would be a happy time as Christmas should be. She knew that Aunt Maude always thought Hamish to be a gormless mouse no matter how well he played the bagpipes.

Maude often remarked: "Now, Dorma, just because he is good with the pipes it does not follow that he is good at everything." Just lately, Dorma was apt to smile secretly to herself when Maude made the remark for the umpteenth time.

During every festive season the McMoosie house would fill with relatives and friends coming and going, laughing, giving presents, opening presents, making sure that the children were entertained and not eating too many of Dorma's homemade, sweet, spicy Christmas pies. It was one of Hamish's "To Do" things that he was responsible for getting in an ample supply of Invercockaleekie Special Reserve damson wine, MacHotts ginger ale, elderberry wine, and a barrel of MacTennant's dandelion beer for those who wanted it. The children had the choice of fizzy mineral waters or fruit juices to wash down their Christmas pies. No doubt that they would have quiet sips from glasses of damson wine when the grown-ups were not looking. It was a very naughty thing to do, but then taking a little tiny sip at Christmas could be forgiven.

Time had passed all too quickly for Hamish, and today was the twenty-third of December, the day when Aunt Maude and her long, black umbrella with the goose-head handle, would arrive from her home in Edzell Castle. Hamish was not at all sure he liked the idea of Aunt Maude staying and for so long – right up until the day after New Year's Day! He muttered to himself that he could probably just about stand Aunt Maude, but her long, black umbrella with the goose-head handle, well, that was another matter. Hamish sometimes felt that the long black umbrella had a mind of its own, but then again he was not sure. One can never tell with umbrellas.

"Oh me," thought Hamish to himself "Aunt Maude for eleven days: double bother, double bother. I feel that this may well be a long, hard winter."

Hamish was sitting on the old red leather sofa, drinking tea and dunking an Abernethy biscuit, looking out at the sky, which seemed to cloud over in harmony with his thoughts about Aunt Maude – a grey, mushy darkish, sort of shade. The frosted window and his icy drawing had all gone

leaving only a slight trickle of water running down the pane. The sky now became darker and tinged with pink behind emerging grey clouds. "Always a sign of snow when the darkening sky is tinged with pink," Hamish remarked to the room.

His thoughts went back to the odd things Dorma had been doing. He thought about the covers she was knitting for his golf clubs . . . why in white? They would be better in a dark green – he liked dark green – and why angora wool?

At the very moment he was in his most deepest thoughts Dorma came in carrying a very large cardboard box that contained the Christmas fairy, an armful of Christmas streamers, coloured paper bells and a Happy Christmas sign.

"Talking to yourself again Hamish? Dear Aunt Maude will be here soon. I forgot the fairy for the top of the tree. Can you put it at the top of the tree for me? I think that it is just a little too high up for me to reach. And please can you put up the decorations and cut some holly from the woods – it is full of berries this year."

Hamish looked down at the cardboard box after Dorma had left the room. He rummaged in the box with one paw and took out the fairy – she looked lovely. To cheer himself up, and to escape from thinking of Aunt Maude, Hamish started to sing a jaunty fisherman's song that he had learned the night previously when practising with the Keltic Moosie Pipe and Fiddle Band. As he sang and hummed, his legs swung back and forth in time with the tune and his right paw, almost without his knowing, picked up the fairy, and tossed it high into the air. Hamish continued tossing the fairy up and down in time with his singing and humming. After a while, Hamish remembered Dorma's instructions and stopped singing the jaunty tune. He sighed and half-heartedly started to get up from the comfortable, old, red leather sofa. As he did so, his legs stopped swinging, but his paw, almost as if it had a mind completely of its own, continued to toss the fairy up and down. The little fairy soared high into the air and was on its way down again when a shrill voice with the chill of the north wind blasted in from the hall.

"Haaaamissshhh! Come here at once! Dorma tells me that you have not yet finished doing the things on your 'To Do' list. She could do with some help about the home."

Aunt Maude and her umbrella had arrived from Edzell Castle.

Hamish was so startled by Aunt Maude's piercing voice, that instead of getting up from the sofa at a nice, leisurely Hamish-pace he shot up much too quickly. His legs went one way and his arms another. The little Christmas fairy, now on its way down and having no paw in which to land, crashed heavily onto the polished wooden floor. There was a feeble pop-like sound as the fragile decoration landed on the floor. Hamish, hoping that his ears had not heard what they had heard, looked down. He hoped that his eyes were not seeing what they were seeing. The fairy was lying in a tangled heap with a broken arm and a broken leg.

"Double bother!" remarked Hamish to the fairy as he picked it up and looked at it more closely. "Whoops, and double bother! And double bother again – I will need some super glue to put this to rights."

There was only one thing to do – he had to hide the fairy, and quickly too, before Dorma and Aunt Maude found out. Hamish gently picked up the pieces, hid them with the other decorations and put the box in his bedroom. Hamish decided that that was the best that he could do for now. He would have to come back later and do a proper job.

"Haaamish!" came the cry from the kitchen.

Right now, Aunt Maude was waiting and one could not keep her waiting for too long.

So far, Hamish's day was not progressing in any way that appealed to him whatsoever. He heard the booming tones of Aunt Maude's voice coming from the kitchen – she was talking about certain folk who left things to the last minute. He opened the door and went in.

"Morning, favourite Aunt. How are you?"

Hamish had left out the "good" of "good morning" as his day was, so far, turning out to be anything but good, and he had a feeling that it might well get worse before getting better.

Aunt Maude peered over the top of her glasses and fixed Hamish with a very un-favourite Aunt type of look.

"Hamish, today is the twenty-third of December. What happens on the twenty-fifth? Christmas day is what happens on the twenty-fifth, is it not?" She had a bad habit of asking questions of folk and then answering them herself.

Hamish nodded frantically. As far as he was concerned, any fool knew that Christmas Day was always on the twenty-fifth of December.

However, if Aunt Maude had insisited, the whole world might have had to accept that Christmas day was on the thirty-first of March, or any other day for that matter. She was that sort of mouse.

Before his aunt had time to say another word, Hamish, summoning up all of his courage, declared that he was about to get started that very minute. He added, quickly, that he had in fact ordered all of the festive drinks and would collect them as soon as he had found a holly tree. He would naturally make sure that there were plenty of berries on the holly. He would then put up the Christmas decorations and decorate the Christmas tree that he had cut down earlier.

Aunt Maude looked at Hamish over the top of her glasses and shook her head in disbelief. Hamish, meanwhile, looked carefully at the paw that held the long, black umbrella with the goose-head handle just in case it began to move in his direction. However, with a loud, "Erumpth, nothing but blether!", Aunt Maude flounced out of the kitchen without a backward glance. Hamish was almost sure that the goose-head handle sneered at him as his aunt swept down the hall like some great ocean liner at full speed.

It was time for Hamish to get to work and he went to the front door and looked out to check the weather. It was pointless going into the woods if the snow was falling. A still, grey, cold December day met his eyes and the strong easterly wind made his whiskers dance. There was a slight mantle of snow on the lawn, but that was nothing to worry about.

He could see no sign of Roderick, the human who owned the old house. Hamish stopped looking out and went to find his long scarf and Wellington boots.

Wrapped in a yellow anorak with a long scarf around his neck and with boots on his feet he was ready to face the December day. Hamish collected his axe from the garden shed and set off into the woods to find the holly. The woods were at the bottom of the big garden beyond the apple trees and not too far to walk. Hamish found a very suitable tree. It was a dark green holly with lots of red berries. It was just the type of holly to please Dorma and Aunt Maude, thought Hamish.

He also found some mistletoe and cut down a big bunch. He then went to pick up the Christmas drinks order and hurried home to decorate the house.

All day, almost without a break, Hamish worked hard and soon the house was looking merry and was festooned with coloured paper chains, twinkling fairy lights, and sprigs of holly and mistletoe.

The tree, placed in a big red bucket and always the centre of attraction, was decorated with glass balls, bells and strings of coloured lights that twinkled. Right on the very top of the tree Hamish remembered to place the fairy.

Hamish decided to himself that it was as well to keep quiet about the slight accident that had befallen the fairy. Even after careful use of some fast-setting glue, one of the fairy's arms did not look quite as it should do. It was slightly bent outwards. As he began to climb down the ladder, after placing the fairy where it should be, he gave one final look. A startled squeak burst from his mouth

"Double bother! Double bother! I've glued the leg on back to front. I will never be able to get it right now. That glue has set hard."

Hamish moved one of the twinkling lights a little to help hide the back-to-front leg, and hoped that as the fairy would be at the top of the tree nobody would notice.

Later, he felt tired but pleased with his work. Even if the fairy looked perhaps just a little odd.

The last thing that Hamish did before calling to Dorma and Aunt Maude was to make sure that the fire was burning brightly, so he put more peat and logs onto the glowing embers. Once he was satisfied that the fire was blazing warmly, Hamish turned off the ceiling lights.

With only the flickering twinkling of the tree lights nobody would notice the fairy – he hoped. Hamish then called for them to come to the sitting room.

Dorma and Aunt Maude had also been working hard all day in the kitchen baking Christmas pies, preparing Scottish trifles, making piles of Dorma's special cheesy nibbles and baking two Dundee cakes. When they came into the sitting room and saw how Christmassy everything looked, even Aunt Maude smiled and quietly remarked: "Well done Hamish, well done."

At the same time, she straightened the fairy on the top of the tree. Hamish gulped, quietly expecting Aunt Maude to say something about the fairy. She then moved one of the glass balls to a different spot she thought to be more attractive, and muttered a satisfied: "There . . ."

She smiled, a strange little smile, and kissed Hamish on the cheek. He had survived. Hamish silently shuddered as a result of the kiss. Aunt Maude always smelt of carbolic soap, umbrellas and lavender, which is a quite peculiar combination. Dorma on the other hand gave Hamish a more acceptable thank you. She gave her husband a big hug and said that his favourite supper was ready and on the kitchen table.

Aunt Maude looked back at the tree – there was something not quite right about the fairy but she could not make out what it was – perhaps it was just the way the tree lights were flickering, but she thought that one of the fairy's arms was bent outwards and the right leg appeared to be facing the wrong way.

When the three wee mice folk went back to the kitchen Hamish saw plates of steaming haggis, mashed neeps and creamed tatties set for three. Dorma made wonderful mashed turnip, or as the Scots say "neeps" and her creamed potatoes were always creamy white, light and buttery.

"A meal fit for a king!" squealed Hamish, delighted in the anticipation of eating the haggis he saw steaming on the plate before his eyes.

Much later, a content and still-very-full-of-haggis-neeps-and-tatties Hamish stretched out in his bed and wiggled first one set of paws and then the other. He sighed a very happy sigh and smiled a little Hamish smile to himself. His pleasant feelings ended sharply when an abrupt scream pierced the air: "Hammmmish!"

Hamish, who had very, very quickly disappeared beneath the tartan-patterned duvet on hearing Aunt Maude's cries, shuddered uneasily beneath the duvet. If Hamish could have seen into the sitting room, his eyes would have met with a very strange sight – Aunt Maude peering at the fairy, now in her paws. Her right arm was waving in the air as if trying to find and grasp hold of her long, black umbrella and was uttering terrible things about Hamish.

"What a complete waste of space that mouse is!"

Hamish heard Dorma rush into the sitting room to see what all the noise was about and to check to see if World War Three had started.

Hamish tunnelled even deeper into the depths of the duvet and to what he hoped was relative safety.

"Double bother, double bother. I should have done a better job on that fairy."

"Hamish are you asleep under there?"

Hamish saw Dorma standing, paws on hips at the bedroom door through a small chink where he had cautiously lifted the duvet, just a little. She was looking very cross.

Dorma was wearing her "Hamish! What have you done?" look. Hamish could see she was tapping her right foot – always a bad sign with Dorma. He gulped a little gulp and made snoring sounds.

Aunt Maude, who had now finished her arm waving and had come into the bedroom, heard a muffled snoring sound coming from somewhere deep down under the tartan duvet.

Hamish continued to make more suitable snoring noises until he heard Dorma leading Aunt Maude away to the guest bedroom.

He also heard Aunt Maude muttering that she would speak severely to Hamish in the morning. Dorma said nothing, and that was what Hamish was worried about. When Dorma was very, very cross she was also very, very quiet.

The next morning Hamish was met with a stony silence from Dorma and Aunt Maude when he came down for breakfast. Dorma plonked down his bowl of porridge on the big kitchen table and returned to the stove to finish cooking breakfast. Hamish ate his porridge, very aware of his aunt's beady brown eyes silently watching him as he lifted every spoonful to his mouth. Hamish said nothing and kept his eyes down, looking at his bowl.

When he had finished his porridge Dorma came over and put his plate of sausages, bacon, black pudding and eggs down with so much force that the sausages jumped at least six inches into the air from the plate. One landed with a very wet splashing noise in Hamish's mug of tea. The other landed with a plop and half buried itself in the butter dish. The bacon crisply slipped quietly onto the table. The black pudding slithered off the plate and hid behind the milk jug, where it hoped it would be safe for a moment. The eggs, being more robust, found the warm breakfast plate to their liking and stayed put. Hamish kept his eyes firmly on the eggs and the plate.

He heard Dorma whisper: "Oh Hamish! How could you?" Then, as if to heap more misery on Hamish, Dorma sighed: "Hamish, your carelessness made me so angry that I have broken my spirtle. So there will be no porridge for you until at least the New Year – I have no time to buy a new one."

Hamish sighed a very quiet sigh to himself. Breakfast without porridge was a thought too horrible to consider.

However, all was back to normal by that afternoon, except that is, for the broken spirtle. Dorma and Aunt Maude were talking to Hamish and the house had an air of jollity about it. Hamish did, however, notice that whenever Aunt Maude was about, she made sure he noticed she was walking with a limp. This was a reminder about the fairy's back-to-front leg.

Relatives and friends came from near and far, lingered for a while, and then went their separate ways, smiling and full of Christmas Eve good cheer. Carol singers holding candlelit lanterns laughed and sang at the front door. They were always rewarded with some of Dorma's hot Christmas pies and wished "a very Happy Christmas".

Later, when the house was peaceful, Hamish mentioned the midnight service. Dorma told him that this year she and Aunt Maude would not be attending.

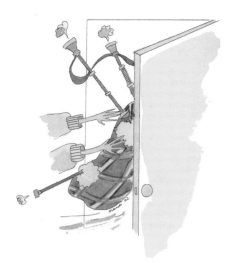

"But Dorma," squeaked Hamish, "you have never missed the Christmas service."

A disapproving look from Aunt Maude was enough to stop Hamish's protests.

"This year is different, dear, and very special," was Dorma's curious reply.

The cathedral bells began to ring out over the silent city at about a quarter to eleven that evening, calling all who wished to attend to come to the midnight service that would welcome in Christmas Day.

Hamish had pulled on his boots and a cosy anorak, wrapped a long tartan scarf about his neck and with his bagpipes tucked under his arm, made his way, alone, through the kirkyard under a deep blue sky, lit only by a crescent moon.

The icy north wind, that had replaced his cousin from the east made itself known to all. The whining, whirling wind that had travelled all the way from the Arctic made folk shiver and think of more snow. Hamish, always prepared for the worst, had looked out at the sky and listened to the wind before setting out. He guessed that there would be thick snow before the night was out but he was warmly dressed and ready.

As Hamish made his way to the cathedral he felt a cold tingle on his whiskers. Then he noticed an eyelash or two began to quiver. He looked up – it had started to snow again. The snow tumbled like icing sugar sieved over Dorma's Christmas pies, and piled in deep, meringue peaks blown by the north wind. When the little mouse entered the majestic old cathedral he found that it was full of chattering, happy folk. A tall, sweet-smelling pine near the door, simply garlanded with hundreds of tiny twinkling lights, glistened like early morning frost. Each of the folk attending the service held a slim lighted candle, illuminating their happy Christmas faces in pools of pale yellow light. Soon it was time for Hamish to play his part in the service and the beautiful, haunting sound of Hamish's bagpipes filled the echoing cathedral with the sweet melody of "Silent Night". It seemed that the very walls of the ancient cathedral stood in awe and wept – maybe it was just the trickle of condensation. Folk passing by outside remarked to each other that the wind sounded like angel's music. Hamish missed not seeing Dorma sitting in her usual place. It was now Christmas Day and it felt less Christmassy without her.

Hamish had much to tell Dorma when he reached home.

"Dorma!" he called as he opened the door, "Dorma?"

"In here, Hamish, with Aunt Maude," called Dorma from their bedroom across the hall.

"Whatever is going on?" thought Hamish, stepping into the softly lit bedroom.

A smiling Dorma sat up in bed, and, snuggled beside her, there were three baby mice, fast asleep.

"Our own wee babies," said Dorma in a kindly but tired voice.

Outside in the dark velvet sky the north star shone brightly and even Aunt Maude had a happy tear glistening in her eye.

"What a Christmas present," sighed Hamish. "To think that I thought you were knitting covers for my golf clubs. Silly me."

"Silly indeed," remarked a smiling Aunt Maude.

From the bed Dorma chuckled to herself. "Golf clubs indeed." Then, smiling she murmured, "oh Hamish."

Hamish, in a moment of uncontrolled happiness, even gave Aunt Maude a kiss.

"A happy Christmas to us and peace for the world – it may not be such a long, hard winter after all."

THE ADVENTURES OF

Hamish McMoosie

Other Titles in This Series

~

HAMISH MCMOOSIE AND THE LONG, BLACK UMBRELLA WITH THE GOOSE-HEAD HANDLE

~

HAMISH MCMOOSIE AND THE MARVELLOUS SET OF NEW BAGPIPES

~

HAMISH MCMOOSIE AND THE QUEST FOR THE NEW SPIRTLE

~